NAPPY
THE
PIRATE BABY

Alan MacDonald

Illustrated by
Elissa Elwick

Barrington Stoke

For Johnny Maynard

Contents

CHAPTER 1

Something Down Below

The *Salty Herring* bobbed like a cork on the sparkling sea. On deck the pirate crew were doing what they loved best: lazing around.

Stinky McFlea snored in a hammock. Irish Stew, the ship's cook, was reading a cook book (*100 Things To Do With Fish*). Long Johns was playing Noughts and Crossbones, while Nitty Nora was knitting herself a stripy swimsuit.

In his cabin, Captain Sprat tried on the smart feather hat he'd bought yesterday when the ship was in port.

All was calm and still until …

"MAA-WAAAH!"

... a strange wailing noise broke the peace.

"What was that?" asked Long Johns.

"I heard it too," said Nitty Nora. "Shh! Listen, mates!"

They all listened hard ...

"MAA-WAAAH!"

There it was again, this time so loud that it woke Stinky McFlea, who fell out of his hammock.

"Maybe it's some sort of fish?" said Irish Stew.

"Like a whale," agreed Stinky McFlea. "A whale that keeps wailing."

"That's no whale," said Nitty Nora. "If you ask me, that be a ghost!"

"Or a huge hungry sea monster that gobbles up pirates," whispered Long Johns.

The cowardly crew turned pale and drew closer together. None of them had ever faced a ghost or a sea monster. Even the sight of a rat sent them running for cover.

The captain came up on deck. He waited for them to admire his smart new hat, but no one did.

"What's going on?" he asked. "You all look like you've seen a ghost."

"Not seen one. We heard one," replied Nitty Nora.

"Or a sea monster," said Long Johns. "It sounded like it came from below."

"Rubbish! You're making it up," scoffed the captain.

"We all heard it, Captain," said Irish Stew.

"Well, if there is anything on board we'll soon find it," said the captain. "Search the ship from top to bottom!"

The crew took mops and rolling pins
to fight off ghosts or monsters and began
to search. They opened hatches, poked in
cupboards and peered under hammocks.
Then they crept below to the store room.
There they heard the wailing again,
which made them all jump.

"MAA-WAAAH!"

"Right then, are we pirates or mice?" said the captain. "One of you open that door."

No one moved.

"Can't *you* open it, Captain?" begged Long Johns.

"I'm the captain, I give the orders," snapped the captain.

The pirates pushed Stinky McFlea to the front. If anything would drive a sea monster away it was the smell of Stinky's feet.

Slowly Stinky turned the handle and the door creaked open. The pirates crept into the dark room, their hearts beating fast.

A strange snuffling sound came from a basket on a shelf.

"Strike me, mates, that's my shopping basket," whispered Irish Stew. "Is the sea monster in there?"

Stinky McFlea lifted the blanket on top of the basket and peeped inside.

"Blow me down!" he cried. "It's a bloomin' baby!"

"A BABY?"

All the pirates crowded round, keen
to see.

There in the basket lay a baby
kicking its chubby legs and looking up at
them with wide blue eyes.

"MAA-WAAAH!" it cried.

CHAPTER 2

Pass the Parcel

None of the pirates knew what to do with a crying baby. They passed the child from one to the other like a parcel.

"Well, do something! Stop his horrible wailing!" cried the captain, putting his fingers in his ears.

Stinky McFlea jiggled the baby on his knee. Long Johns tickled his toes, while Irish Stew pulled funny faces. It made no difference – the baby went on crying.

"MAA-WAAAH! MAA-WAAAH!"

It was Nitty Nora who got to the bottom of the problem.

"Look, he's all wet, poor tiddler!" she said. "He needs a clean nappy."

It took four of them, a sheet of sailcloth and a lot of safety pins, but in the end they got it done.

"There, that's better, isn't it, Baby?" smiled Nitty Nora.

"We can't call him 'Baby'. He needs a name," said Irish Stew.

"How about Nappy?" said Stinky McFlea.

They all agreed that Nappy was the perfect name for a baby.

"Never mind all that," the captain grumbled. "What are we going to do with him?"

None of them knew, so the captain called a ship's meeting. They all squashed into his tiny cabin, which was crammed with maps, sea chests and hats of all shapes and sizes.

The captain spoke first.

"Babies is all well and good," he said. "But we are pirates, not bloomin' babysitters. We can't be running up and down all day looking after a little one."

"Oh but, Captain, he's so *sweet*!" pleaded Stinky McFlea.

"Yes, look at his tiny little fingers and toesies," cooed Irish Stew.

"Don't be so soft! What use is a baby?" argued the captain. "He can't even obey orders!"

Nitty Nora took Nappy in her arms.

"Well, I say we keep the little lad and bring him up like a proper pirate," she said.

"Very well then, we'll take a vote," said the captain. "All in favour of keeping the boy, raise your hand."

All of the crew shot up their hands.

"All against?" said the captain, and waved his own hand in the air.

"AHAAR! We win seven to one!" cried Stinky McFlea, who'd never learned to count.

"All right, have it your own way, but don't say I didn't warn you," moaned the captain. "A baby on board will be nothing but trouble."

CHAPTER 3

Baby on Board

As it turned out, the captain couldn't have been more wrong. From the moment they found Nappy, the pirates took to him as if he was their own. They loved the way Nappy gurgled and giggled when they tickled his tummy or played peek-a-boo.

Nitty Nora knitted him a pirate baby-grow with matching black booties. Irish Stew rigged up a little hammock and fed him milk from a bottle he'd found in the basket. Long Johns took the baby up to the crow's nest and taught him how to look through a telescope. Meanwhile Stinky McFlea sat for hours on deck teaching Nappy how to speak like a proper pirate.

"Say: 'AHARR!'"

"Hee! Hee!" gurgled Nappy.

As for the captain, he pretended he wasn't interested in bloomin' babies. All the same he smiled to himself as he watched the crew playing with Nappy. He had to admit that having a baby on board made the ship a happier place.

*

But that evening, the pirates got a surprise. They were all sitting down to supper when Nappy woke up and began to cry again.

"MAA-WAAAH! MAA-WAAAH!"

"Oh lawks, did you change his nappy?" asked Long Johns.

"Course I did, I'm not daft," said Nitty Nora. "And it's high time you learned to do it."

"Maybe he's hungry, poor tiddler," said Irish Stew. "I'll try giving him some more milk."

But Nappy didn't want any milk. He cried even louder.

"MAA-WAAAH!"

Suddenly the captain sat up. "Oh my stars! We're a pack of fools!" he cried.

"How's that?" asked Stinky.

"Don't you see, you blockheads?" said the captain. "It's not 'Ma-waah' he keeps saying, it's 'Ma-mma'! The poor lad is crying for his mamma!"

The crew looked at each other. The truth was they hadn't even thought about Nappy's mother.

"Maybe he doesn't have a ma," said Stinky.

"Everyone has a ma," said Long Johns. "But how we find her – that's another matter."

The captain pulled at his beard.

"One thing's for sure," he said. "That baby needs his ma, and if he doesn't stop crying he'll give me a thumping headache. Turn the ship around, mates, we're heading back to port!"

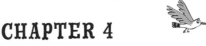

CHAPTER 4

Follow the Basket

Back in port, the pirates trooped down the gangplank and looked around. It was eleven in the morning and the town was noisy and crowded. Finding Nappy's mother wasn't going to be easy.

"So where do we start?" asked Long Johns.

"Maybe we should ask if anyone's lost a baby," said Irish Stew.

"Don't be daft, that'll take for ever!" said the captain. "No, we need to use our brains and think of a clever plan."

The pirates scratched their heads as they tried to think. Stinky McFlea

thought of what he'd like for breakfast
(ham and eggs).

"Wait, I've got it!" cried the captain.
"We just follow the basket."

The crew all looked at Nappy's basket,
but it didn't seem to be going anywhere.

"How do you mean?" asked Nitty
Nora.

"It's plain as paint," said the captain. "When we found Nappy, he was lying in that basket, so the question is how did he get there?"

The pirates had no idea.

"Think back, mates," said the captain. "Last time we were in port, did any of you bring a basket ashore?"

"Oh yes, I did!"

It was Stinky McFlea who'd answered.

"You told me to wash all our smelly socks, Captain," he said. "So I put them in a basket and took them off to wash."

"Now we're getting somewhere," said the captain. "And what did you do with the basket?"

Stinky rubbed his chin. "Ah, there's a question. I remember stopping at the inn for a glass or two while the socks were drying on the sea wall. And when I came back the basket had gone."

"Barnacles!" muttered the captain.

"Hang on a minute, I took it!" said Long Johns.

Ye Olde Shipwreck

Ye Olde Shipwreck

PIRATES ONLY

LOST PARROT

WANTED

WANTED

ye olde library

Port

ye olde market

"You did?" said Nitty Nora.

"Yes, I was catching crabs from the dock and I needed a basket to put them in," said Long Johns. "I saw it lying on the ground, so I borrowed it."

"Oh ho! And you filled it with crabs?" said the captain.

"Well, no," replied Long Johns.

"You just said you did!" cried the captain.

"I was going to, but then I ran into Irish Stew," explained Long Johns. "He said he needed the basket in a hurry, like."

They all turned to Irish Stew.

"Well, it was my basket in the first place," the cook said crossly. "I never said people could put their smelly socks or crabs in it."

The captain tried to keep his temper.

"Never mind the socks! All I want to know is: *what happened to the bloomin' basket?*" he shouted.

"That's easy – I took it to the market," Irish Stew told him. "We needed potatoes and carrots."

"Did you buy some?" asked the captain.

"Of course I did," said Irish Stew. "I got a good price from the woman at the market stall too. And now I remember, she had a basket just like mine."

The captain clapped a hand to his head.

"You dozy dogfish!" he groaned. "That's what happened – you picked up the wrong basket! Instead of potatoes you brought back a bloomin' baby!"

"Oops! Silly me!" said Irish Stew.

CHAPTER 5

Raining Potatoes

There was no time to lose. The market took place every morning, but it closed at noon.

The pirates rushed to the square. Were they too late?

Nappy woke up, so Long Johns tucked him under one big arm.

"This woman, what did she look like?" asked Nitty Nora.

"Don't ask me," said Irish Stew. "Like a woman who sells potatoes."

At last they came out into the market place. Rows of stalls were selling fruit, fish and more fish, along with lamps, ropes and nets. The pirates walked past the stalls and looked for one selling potatoes. At last they found it, but the owner had a thick black beard and an eye patch.

"Blow me! I hope that's not the baby's mother," whispered Stinky McFlea.

Just then a woman with bright red hair came running up.

"That's them!" she cried, and pointed a finger at the pirates. "They're the dirty, stinking scoundrels that stole my baby!"

The captain was about to protest, but he didn't get the chance. A potato hit him on the head and knocked off his new hat. The woman hurled potatoes like rocks and one struck Stinky McFlea on the nose.

"OUCH!"

"Take cover, lads, we're under fire!" cried the captain.

The crew didn't wait for orders – they'd already hidden under tables.

The captain grabbed his hat and dived behind a crate of fish. When he peeped out again, a carrot flew past his ear.

This is ridiculous, he thought, *we're being attacked by vegetables!*

He took out his white hanky and waved it in the air.

"Cease fire!" he shouted. "We surrender!"

"What have you done with my baby?" the woman called out.

Long Johns lifted Nappy high into the
air to show he was safe.

"Tommy!" cried his mother.

"MA-WAAAH!" wailed Nappy.

*

The battle was over and Nappy was soon back in his mother's arms. She told them her name was Molly. When she heard their story, she said sorry for calling them dirty, stinking scoundrels.

"We never meant to steal the lad," said Irish Stew. "I must have picked up your basket by mistake."

The captain swept off his hat and bowed low.

"Dear lady, may I offer my humble apologies," he said, and kissed Molly's hand. She blushed – no one had ever called her a lady before.

*

At last it was time for the pirates to return to the *Salty Herring*. They took it in turns to say goodbye to Nappy.

"You be good, little one, and remember all we taught you," sniffed Stinky McFlea.

They trailed off down the street, stopping to dab their eyes and blow their noses.

"We'll never ever see him ever again!
Boo hoo hoo!" sobbed Long Johns.

CHAPTER 6

Shipmates All

Back on the *Salty Herring*, the crew got ready to set sail.

"It won't be the same without him," sighed Stinky McFlea. "I'm going to miss the little lad."

Irish Stew nodded. "Me too. I loved singing him to sleep."

"He would have made a proper pirate too," said Nitty Nora.

The captain stared out to sea. It must have been the wind that stung his eyes, making them water. Still, they'd done the right thing, he thought, a baby belonged with his mother.

"Right, look lively, mates!" he cried. "And no more sighing and snivelling. Are we pirates or a bunch of milksops?"

They raised the anchor and hoisted the main sail. But just as they were about to pull up the gangplank, Long Johns spotted someone on the dock.

"Strike me, mates! Who's this?" he cried.

It was Molly and she was running towards them with Nappy in his basket.

The captain came to the ship's rail.

"Well?" he said. "Did we forget something?"

"I wanted to ask you one question," panted Molly, when she got her breath back. "What if I was to join you? I'm tired of working in the market every day and smelling of potatoes. Besides, since I was a girl I've always dreamed of going to sea."

The captain stroked his beard. "You'd have to become a pirate and take orders," he warned.

"I don't mind that. You seem like very nice pirates," said Molly. "You don't steal or swear or fight battles, do you?"

"Oh no," said Stinky McFlea. "We sometimes play cards and eat biscuits, but that's all."

"There's just one thing," said Molly. "I'd have to bring my baby along – is that all right?"

The pirates grinned. All right? They'd be over the moon! They'd have Nappy back and they could go on teaching him to be a proper pirate.

"Let's vote on it, mates," said the captain. "All those in favour say, 'Aye!'"

"AYE!" shouted the pirates all together.

"Welcome aboard, then, Molly," laughed the captain, and threw his new feather hat high into the air. A gust of wind caught it and it landed in the sea.

"AHAARR!" giggled Nappy.

Our books are tested
for children and young people by
children and young people.

Thanks to everyone who consulted on
a manuscript for their time and effort in
helping us to make our books better
for our readers.

First published in 2021 in Great Britain by
Barrington Stoke Ltd
18 Walker Street, Edinburgh, EH3 7LP

www.barringtonstoke.co.uk

A CIP catalogue record for this book is available
from the British Library upon request

ISBN: 978-1-78112-941-8

Printed by Hussar Books, Poland

This book is in a super-readable format for young readers
beginning their independent reading journey.